The Mysterious Key

Level 11 – Lime

D1646409

LON   NET

Helpful Hints for Reading at Home

The focus phonemes (units of sound) used throughout this series are in line with the order in which your child is taught at school. This offers a consistent approach to learning whether reading at home or in the classroom.

HERE ARE SOME COMMON WORDS THAT YOUR CHILD MIGHT FIND TRICKY:

water	where	would	know	thought	through	couldn't
laughed	eyes	once	we're	school	can't	our

TOP TIPS FOR HELPING YOUR CHILD TO READ:

- Encourage your child to read aloud as well as silently to themselves.
- Allow your child time to absorb the text and make comments.
- Ask simple questions about the text to assess understanding.
- Encourage your child to clarify the meaning of new vocabulary.

This book focuses on developing independence, fluency and comprehension. It is a lime level 11 book band.

The Mysterious Key

Written by
Mignonne Gunasekara

Illustrated by
Farah Shah

Chapter One

Lost and Found

Cara's grandparents loved car boot sales. And they loved them even more when they could take Cara along with them. The sun shone down on the three of them as they wandered through the various stalls of bric-a-brac, looking for a bargain.

Grandma had made it some way ahead when Grandpa tapped Cara's arm and whispered in her ear.

"I want to get your grandma something as special as she is," he said. "Can you help me choose something she'd like?"

"Of course, Grandpa," Cara whispered back. "I'll keep an eye out for something really special!"

She looked at the tables nearby. There were some scarves, but Grandma had so many already. There were some DVDs, but Grandma didn't like sitting still for too long. Cara was looking at some statues when she saw something glittering out of the corner of her eye. She turned to see a beautiful old jewellery box, partly hidden by an old aquarium.

"Grandpa, what about that jewellery box?" asked Cara.

"What a good find," said Grandpa. "Grandma will really love that! Let's get it for her." Grandpa bought the jewellery box and Cara put it in her backpack. Just then, Grandma reappeared.

"What are you two up to?" she asked.

"Nothing!" said Cara and Grandpa.

When they had finished their shopping and got home, Grandpa decided that it was time for Grandma's surprise.

"Close your eyes," he said. "Cara and I have something for you."

Grandma covered her eyes and Cara pulled the box from her bag.

"You can open your eyes now!" said Cara.

Grandma peeked out from behind her hands and a smile lit up her face. "Wow, it's beautiful," she gasped. "But it's not my birthday yet!"

"We don't need to wait for your birthday to remind you how special you are," said Cara.

"Thank you very much," said Grandma, as she gave Cara and Grandpa a big hug. "Let's open it!"

Grandma lifted the lid while Cara and Grandpa looked inside. The box should have been empty, but inside was a lonely key. "I hope that doesn't open anything important," said Grandpa.
"I'm sure it doesn't, or it would have been missed before now," said Grandma. "This is very old. And there's no point in keeping keys that don't open anything."

Grandma was just about to throw the key away when a little voice at the back of Cara's mind told her that this was a very important key.

"Can I please have the key, Grandma?" she asked.

"Of course you can, Cara," said Grandma. "I suppose it is a very pretty key."

Grandma handed Cara the key, and Cara took a closer look at it. It was gold with a leafy design. It was beautiful! Cara put it in her pocket. It had to open something, and she could not wait to find out what.

Over the next few days, Cara carried the key with her everywhere. She tried every lock she thought it would fit.

Letterboxes, the fancy-dress costume chest in her classroom, every locked door she passed... Cara tried them all, but nothing opened. Some of the other kids were starting to laugh at her, but Cara didn't mind.

She had her own special quest and they were the ones missing out, even if they didn't know it. She just wished her quest wasn't taking so long to complete.

Feeling a little sad that she hadn't unlocked anything yet, Cara walked home from school in a bad mood.

She was in a hurry to get back and curl up with her grandparents and a nice book, so she decided to take a shortcut through the park. The wind swirled autumn leaves around her, and Cara started to walk faster.

But then, as Cara passed a very large, old, knobbly tree, the key started to rattle in her pocket!

"What on earth is happening?" thought Cara. "The key has come to life!"

She took four steps forward and one step back until she worked out that the tree was making the key do this.

She took the key out of her pocket and walked towards the tree. The closer she got to the tree, the faster the key shook, until it started humming a beautiful song.

"It's like the tree is calling me," muttered Cara. "How strange..."

Cara followed the pull of the key and walked round to the back of the tree.

There, hidden by some branches, was a door she'd never seen before.

"Finally!" yelled Cara. "This has to be it! This has to be what this key opens!"

She tried the key in the door's lock and of course, it fit like a glove. She heard the latch click open. With a creak, the door swung outwards, and Cara stepped into the darkness inside...

Chapter Two

Wake Up

She didn't get more than a few steps in before she bumped into something. Out of the darkness opened a pair of huge, gleaming, amber eyes. They stared straight back at her, not an inch from her face. Cara screamed, and so did the person she had bumped into!

As she scrambled backwards to get out of the tree trunk, the mysterious person ran out alongside her.

She saw him clearly now. Someone who appeared to be a boy around her own age stood in front of her. But he couldn't be any ordinary boy, because out of the mop of curly hair on his head poked a pair of pointy ears!

"Who are you?" he huffed, out of breath from the fright he'd just had.

"I could ask you the same question!" said Cara. "Or more importantly, what are you?"

"That's a bit rude," he said, wrinkling his nose. "I didn't ask what you were, although you're clearly no pixie."

"You're a pixie?" exclaimed Cara. "That's so cool. I'm a human, if you know what that is?" "Of course I know about humans," he said. "I've just never met one before." "And I've never met a pixie before," said Cara. "My name's Cara, what's yours?" "Idris," he replied, and the name sounded like sunshine and honey in Cara's ears.

"What were you doing standing about in the dark on your own, Idris?" asked Cara.

"I— Well, I was playing hide and seek with my friends," said Idris. "But I must have fallen asleep because the next thing I remember is you."

"So, your friends must be nearby?" asked Cara.

"I don't know," he said. "Time doesn't move in the same way for pixies as it does for humans. My friends could be anywhere by now."

"What do you mean?" asked Cara. "How can time move differently? Time is time."

"A thousand years is a long time for you," explained Idris. "But it's the blink of an eye for me."

"But if time has moved more quickly for you, they can't have gone far," said Cara.

"They may have had to," said Idris, and Cara followed his gaze over her shoulder to the town behind them. "This place has changed so much; I don't know where they could be. I don't even know where I am anymore. Not really."

"I can help you find them," offered Cara. "I know this town like the back of my hand."

"That's very kind of you," said Idris. "But I think I can manage."

"Oh, it's no bother," said Cara. "I want to help."

Idris saw that Cara was not going to back down.

"Fine," he sighed. "You're a stubborn one, I see."

"I'm not stubborn," said Cara. "I get things done."

"Alright, Cara-Who-Gets-Things-Done," said Idris. "Take me home."

"Well, we need to find something in this town that hasn't changed in a thousand years," said Cara, as she began to lead Idris out of the park. "Then you can work out where you're going, can't you?"

"That sounds like a good plan," said Idris. "Do you know where the oldest part of town is?"

"I think so," replied Cara. "The old clock in the town centre. That's been there longer than anyone can remember."

"That will be the best place to start," said Idris. "Let's go."

The two of them marched off into the autumn afternoon.

Chapter Three

The Way Back

Cara and Idris had made it out of the park and were nearly at the town centre. They could see the old clock in the distance. They just needed to cross two more streets and they'd be there. As they waited for the crossing light to turn green, two kids came around the corner, sucking on lollipops.

They were the kids who had been making fun of Cara at school.

"Oh no," said Cara. "Not them."

"Do you know them?" asked Idris.

"They're just some kids from my school," she replied. "They were teasing me earlier, but it's fine. Just ignore them if they come this way."

"Teasing?" asked Idris. "What kind of teasing? Were they joking?"

"Not really," said Cara. "They laughed at me, but the joke is on them. They are the ones missing out on meeting you."

"They laughed at you?" asked Idris. "That's not kind!"

Idris started to stare at the kids with clenched fists. Cara heard a crackling sound. It was coming from Idris's hands! Little sparks of electricity danced between his fingers.

"Let's teach them a little lesson that kindness costs nothing," said Idris.
He opened his hands, and the sparks shot to the ground. In front of Cara, the autumn leaves started to swirl and crunch. They zoomed towards the mean kids and started piling up around them.
"Ahh!" yelled the kids. "What's happening?"

The leaves kept swirling and swirling until the kids were completely covered in them! Then Idris wrinkled his nose, and just like that, the leaves all dropped. The kids slowly crawled out of the leaf pile. There were leaves in their hair, leaves in their clothes and leaves stuck to their lollipops. They couldn't eat those anymore.

The crossing light turned green and started beeping. It was safe to cross the road. Cara grabbed Idris's hand and the two of them crossed the road, giggling.

"Idris!" said Cara. "What if someone had seen you?"

"It was the wind," said Idris. "What else could it have been?"

"Pixie magic," whispered Cara.

"Shhh," hushed Idris. "That stays between us."

They walked for some time, then turned the corner and came face to face with the clock. It towered above the two of them. The hands of the clock had stopped moving long ago, but it was still beautiful. At its base was a huge plaque.

"It says it was built in 1306," said Cara.

"We need something older than that," said Idris.

"Sorry," said Cara. "I think that's as old as it gets."

As they both stared up at the clock, trying to think of what to do next, the Sun set just a little lower in the sky. Suddenly, a ray of light hit the clock's glass face, and bounced back in a beautiful rainbow that stretched over the whole town.

Built in
1306

Built i
1306

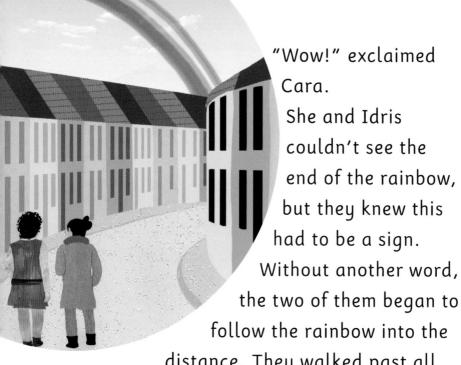

"Wow!" exclaimed Cara.

She and Idris couldn't see the end of the rainbow, but they knew this had to be a sign. Without another word, the two of them began to follow the rainbow into the distance. They walked past all the shops, past all the houses and right to the edge of town.

"Where is it taking us?" thought Cara.

Cara was about to say something when it finally appeared. The end of the rainbow landed not in a pot of gold, but at the foot of a very old tree.

"Race you there!" shouted Idris, and he took off running towards the tree. Cara was not about to be left behind, so she ran after him.

By the time she caught up with him, Idris was halfway up the tree.

"What are you doing?" she called up to him.

"Trying to get a better view!" he replied.

"Be careful!" said Cara. "It's a long way down."

"Not for a pixie," said Idris, cheekily.

Cara thought for a minute.

"Wait, does that mean you can fly?" she asked.

Idris didn't reply.

"Idris?" called Cara. "Are you OK?"

After a moment of silence that lasted a heartbeat too long, Cara heard whooping coming from the leaves above. Idris dropped down in front of her in a flurry of leaves.

"I saw Fay Hill!" he cheered. "I know where I am!"

"That's great news!" exclaimed Cara. "What's Fay Hill?"

"It's where we'll find the doorway to my world," said Idris. "And now I know how to get there. Follow me!"

Idris took off into the woods.

"Wait for me!" called Cara, chasing after him.

"Sorry," said Idris over his shoulder. "I'm just excited because we're so close!"

Idris slowed so that he and Cara were now running together.

They emerged from the other side of the trees into fields that spread out as far as they could see. But there was something different about these fields. The grass was a little too green. The flowers were a little too perfect. And there were no bugs in sight. They must have been getting close to something magical.

"Come on," said Idris, and he set off across the fields. Cara could see what she guessed was Fay Hill. As they reached the top of the hill, Cara saw a giant tree stump. It was wider than any tree she'd ever seen. The edges of the stump were carved with beautiful swirling patterns.

"This is the portal to the pixie world," said Idris. "All the clues led me right where I needed to go."

"Your friends must have left them for you," said Cara.

"Yes," whispered Idris. "They must have."

He turned to face Cara. It was time to say goodbye. He was going to miss his new friend, but home was calling.

"I have to go now, Cara," he said. "But as a goodbye gift, I would like you to have the tree."

"I couldn't-" Cara began to say.

Idris handed Cara the key to the tree.

"It's yours now," he said. "Look after it well. I hope it brings you lots of fun and happiness."

"Thank you," said Cara. She was sure that it would.

"Goodbye, Cara," said Idris. "Thank you for helping me find my way home."

"Goodbye, Idris," said Cara. "It was nice to meet you."

"It was nice to meet you, too," he said. "And remember, a pixie never forgets a friend." Idris turned and stepped onto the tree stump. There was a flash of light and then he was gone...

Epilogue

After

By the following weekend, Cara had turned the tree into a secret den. It was cosy, and bright, with hundreds of fairy lights on the walls. Cara had pulled an armchair inside and set up a reading snug in the corner. This was her space now. And it would forever remind her of her magical encounter with a very special pixie.

The Mysterious Key

1. What locks did Cara try to put the key in?

2. When was the town clock built?

3. Where did the end of the rainbow land?

   (a) At the foot of a very old tree

   (b) In a pot of gold

   (c) At the foot of the town clock

4. What was at the top of Fay Hill?

5. How do you think Cara felt about the kids teasing her at school? Do you think she should have told a grown-up? Why?

©2020 **BookLife Publishing Ltd.**
King's Lynn, Norfolk PE30 4LS

ISBN 978-1-83927-027-7

All rights reserved. Printed in Malaysia.
A catalogue record for this book is available
from the British Library.

The Mysterious Key
Written by Mignonne Gunasekara
Illustrated by Farah Shah

An Introduction to BookLife Readers...

Our Readers have been specifically created in line with the London Institute of Education's approach to book banding and are phonetically decodable and ordered to support each phase of the Letters and Sounds document.

Each book has been created to provide the best possible reading and learning experience. Our aim is to share our love of books with children, providing both emerging readers and prolific page–turners with beautiful books that are guaranteed to provoke interest and learning, regardless of ability.

BOOK BAND GRADED using the Institute of Education's approach to levelling.

PHONETICALLY DECODABLE supporting each phase of Letters and Sounds.

EXERCISES AND QUESTIONS to offer reinforcement and to ascertain comprehension.

BEAUTIFULLY ILLUSTRATED to inspire and provoke engagement, providing a variety of styles for the reader to enjoy whilst reading through the series.

AUTHOR INSIGHT:
MIGNONNE GUNASEKARA

Despite being BookLife Publishing's newest recruit, Mignonne Gunasekara has already written fourteen books about everything from starter science and disastrous deaths throughout history to dinosaurs.
Born in Sri Lanka, Mignonne has always been drawn to stories, whether they are told through literature, film or music. After studying Biomedical Science at King's College London, Mignonne completed a short course in screenwriting at the National Centre for Writing in Norwich, during which she explored writing scripts for the different mediums of film, theatre and radio.

This book focuses on developing independence, fluency and comprehension. It is a lime level 11 book band.